For my muse, who keeps me from getting too serious.
And to Sue—for seriously everything!
—J. P.

For Florence
—D. R.

GREENWILLOW BOOKS

THIS IS A SERIOUS BOOK

BY Jodie Parachini   ILLUSTRATED **BY Daniel Rieley**

GREENWILLOW BOOKS
An Imprint of HarperCollinsPublishers

This is a serious book.

Everything in this book is
thoughtful, proper, respectable,
and, of course, very, *very* serious.

Nothing silly is allowed.

Here is a list of things that are not allowed in this book:

funny faces,

back handsprings,

dressing up,

jumping up and down.

And definitely no tooting.

Excuse me.

This means you.

Quiet!

A serious book would never have anything ridiculous in it,

like ducky pajamas . . .

or unicycles.

Also, a serious book must be black and white.

Ahem!

This means you.

Wait a minute . . . who are *you*?

Yes, you're black and white, but you're not serious!

If you two are going to stay in this book,
you need to be serious. Try pretending you're at a museum.

No!
Not like that.

Okay, try pretending you're in a library.

No!

Shhh!

Who are *you*?

ss*s* s s s s s ssilly

Go away!

This is a serious book!

This isn't working.

I'm sorry. You're all going to have to leave immediately.

A serious book isn't silly—it explains things.

Now, where was I?

Hello?

Now there's a penguin?

I told you all to leave, not to have a parade!

Please!

No. More. Animals.

Monkeys?

No!
Absolutely not!
A serious book never, ever has monkeys.
And that's final!

Now what's going on?

Hey! Don't do that!

Okay,
I give up.

Do whatever you want.

Have a party.

Sing, swing, eat cake!

Dance on the ceiling.

Write your own book.

This book is a . . .

NOT SO serious book!

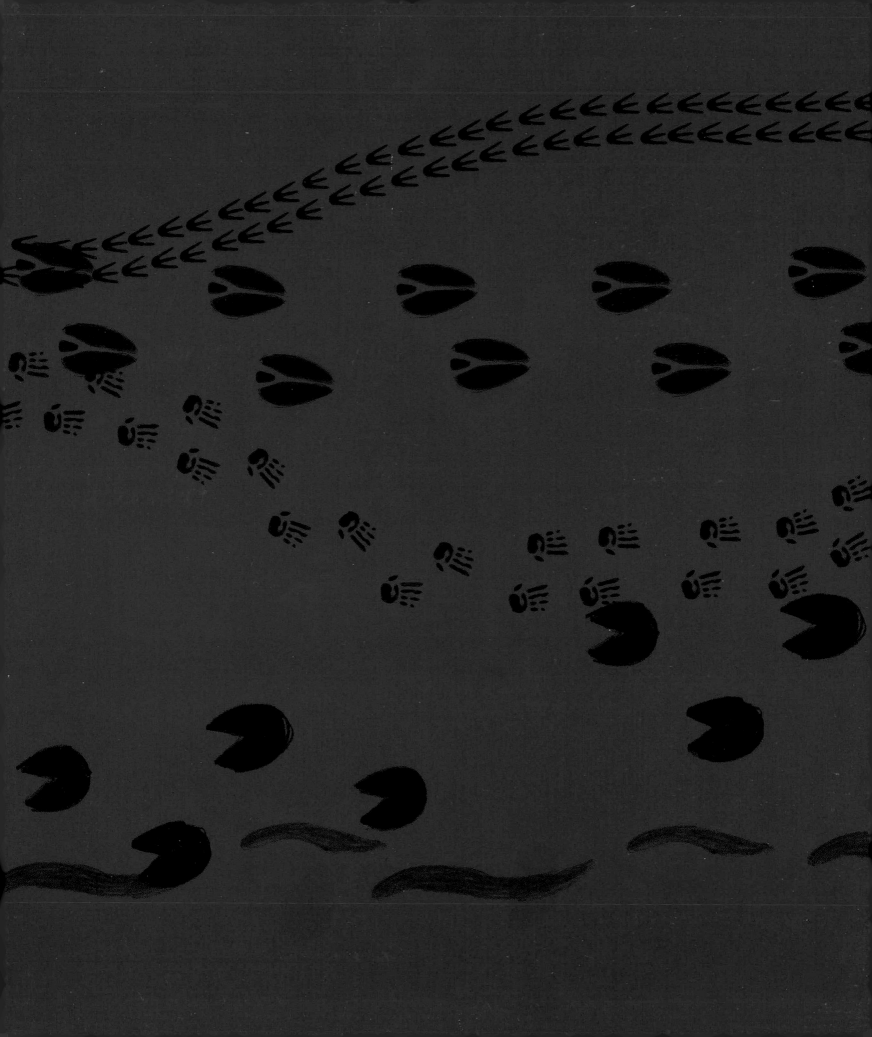